LOGGERS

Volume 7

Tales of the Wild West Series

Rick Steber

Illustrations by Don Gray

NOTE
Loggers is the seventh book in the
Tales of the Wild West Series.

Loggers
Volume 7
Tales of the Wild West Series

Bonanza Publishing
Box 204
Prineville, Oregon 97754

INTRODUCTION

Logging in North America began with the arrival of European colonists in the 1600s. In a few short decades there were water-powered sawmills scattered up and down the eastern seaboard with the main concentration in northern New England. The lumber was used to build ships, furniture, kegs and barrels, buggies and wagons. As the loggers cleared areas in the forest, others arrived to farm the ground.

It took 200 years for the timber to be logged from the eastern seaboard. The loggers and lumbermen moved inland to the Great Lakes region and when they had high graded the timber there, they continued west to northern California and the Pacific Northwest.

Lumberman Samuel Wilkeson wrote in 1869, on viewing the Western forests for the first time, "Oh! What timber! These trees so enchain the sense of the grand and so enchant the sense of the beautiful that I am loth to depart. Forests in which you cannot ride a horse -- forests into which you cannot see, and which are almost dark under a bright midday sun -- such forests containing firs, cedars, pine, spruce and hemlock -- forests surpassing the woods of all the rest of the globe in their size, quantity and quality of the timber. Here can be found great trees, monarchs to whom all worshipful men inevitably lift their hats."

VIRGIN FOREST

The American colonists found themselves at the edge of what seemed to be an endless forest stretching west across the North American continent. They made use of the trees, cutting them to clear fields and build log cabins, and burning firewood for cooking and heating.

Within a few years sawmills were built at Jamestown, Virginia and on the Saco River in Maine. Maine was particularly well-suited for commercial logging and soon sailing ships built of Maine wood were exporting pine and spruce lumber to Europe and the West Indies.

Whitewater logging became the standard technique to harvest the timber. Through the winter logs were cut and dragged by teams of oxen or horses to the banks of frozen streams. In the spring loggers rolled the logs into the water and sent them downstream in spectacular drives.

Invariably, at narrow points along the way the logs would jam. Daring men would walk the dangerous pile of logs and use long-handled, steel-tipped pike poles to free logs and break the jam that dammed the river. When the key log was freed the men ran for their lives.

Lumber barons harvested the best timber and turned their attention southward, into upstate New York. With completion of the Erie Canal in 1825 Albany, the canal's eastern terminus, became the hub of the busiest lumber market in the world.

In a few short decades the local timber was cut and the lumber barons moved to the Great Lakes region. When that vast supply began to dwindle, their attention shifted to the Pacific Northwest. This richly-timbered land would, according to the lumbermen, provide them forever with "a truly inexhaustible supply of logs."

PAUL AND BABE

Paul Bunyan was a giant lumberjack, a descendant of mountain men, and the folklore hero of the Great Lakes states. After the timber in that region was harvested Paul and his faithful companion Babe, the Blue Ox, came to the Northwest.

According to legend, one day Paul and Babe went for a walk. Paul dragged his peavey along the ground for a while and the result was the Columbia River Gorge. Paul fell trees by swinging an ax around his head. Occasionally he would swing a three-mile-long crosscut saw -- the same one he used to comb his hair -- to mow down whole sections of the forest.

An oldtimer once told the bunkhouse tale of how Paul Bunyan and Babe dealt with a log jam. "Paul and Babe were driving logs when they jammed at a narrow part of the river. Logs were piled five hundred feet deep and backed up ten miles.

"Paul brought Babe around to the head of the jam. He positioned the ox just so and then he got off to one side, brought out his rifle, a 30.30 Winchester, and fired at Babe's backside. Babe, thinking flies were stinging him, began switching his tail. The wind created by the switching pushed the logs back upstream. That freed the jam."

The first Paul Bunyan story appeared in the Detroit *News* in 1910. The second was a poem which appeared in *American Lumberman* in 1914. The legend grew with loggers inventing exploits and telling their stories in logging camp bunkhouses. Storytellers related how Paul became the boss of an entire race of hybrid loggers. One tale had it that the runt of the men broke his leg one winter -- five feet below the knee.

The mightiest logger the world has ever known never died. After he had gone from coast to coast cutting down the forest he and Babe simply retired. They are alive to this day and living somewhere in the Alaskan bush.

INDIAN LOGGERS

The Indians of the Northwest practiced forest management long before the white man coined the term. They used fire to open up the forest for semi-cultivated crops like huckleberries, roots and tobacco. Their fires naturally fertilized the soil and helped to clear underbrush from the forest floor.

Coastal Indians were first to log the huge trees of the region. Using stone hatchets and sharpened shells they bore holes in the trunk of a towering cedar or spruce and built fires in the holes. In time the undermined tree would topple. They steamed the wood to make it more malleable and hacked and burned the log to craft intricate canoes up to 70 feet in length. James Swan, who chronicled Indian life on the Northwest coast for the Smithsonian Institution, reported in the 1860s, "These canoes are beautifully modeled, resembling in their bows our finest clipper ships." He also noted that the great canoes were equipped with sails made of woven bark strips and that they were taken far out to sea where the Indians harpooned whales.

The Indians also fell trees, usually western red cedar, and carved elaborate totem poles in the likeness of animals, birds and mythical creatures. They believed these totems protected them and brought them good luck.

Tribes of the interior also practiced logging and canoe making. They hand-crafted small canoes, most were 15 to 25 feet in length, from a variety of trees including cottonwood, sugar pine and ponderosa pine. Canoes were important as the rivers and lakes were their highways. In addition to transportation the Indians also used the canoes for fishing and hunting.

THE FIRST SAWMILL

One day in 1631 colonists watched the unloading of the English ship *Pied Cowe*. From the hold was removed a strange-looking piece of machinery -- wooden wheels, a wooden frame, iron connecting rods and a long saw with jagged teeth. This was the first sawmill brought to the New World.

The colonists had already constructed a dam across the Salmon Falls River, in what would become the state of Maine, and installed a large waterwheel on the millrace at the lower end. When the sawmill was in place two men rolled a log onto the carriage, clamped it in with iron dogs and gave the signal for the sluice gate to be opened. Water rushed down the millrace and over the wheel. The big wheel groaned and slowly turned on its axle.

The sawyer pulled an iron lever and the saw moved up and down. He pulled another lever and the pine log moved to meet the saw. The saw whined, sawdust flew as the hungry teeth bit into the log and the air was charged with the rich perfume of pine -- an aroma once smelled, never forgotten.

The saw settled into a steady swish-swish, moving up and down as the carriage pushed the log into the teeth. The first cut was made and the carriage returned and again started forward. Within a few short moments the first board, gleaming milk-white, fell away from the log. The small crowd cheered.

From this humble beginning sawmills ripped through the magnificent forests that covered the continent. And in less than 300 years the seemingly endless expanse of timber had been manufactured into lumber that built a nation.

BEST TIMES

"I was a high climber, glamour boy of the woods," related Harold Morgan of Junction City, Oregon.

"Been almost fifty years since I went up a tree but I remember it like it was yesterday. Buckle on spurs and belt, tie on the topping saw and ax, start up. The bark is soft. Throw up the rope. Climb. Throw up the rope. Climb. Cut off limbs as you come to them. Sweat rolls. One hundred and eighty feet up the tree is still twenty inches in diameter. Pause to get your breath, look out over the country. Wonderful view. Yarder looking small. Wave to the rigging crew, they wave back. They will be watching.

"Start the undercut same as if you were on the ground, oiling the saw from a small bottle of kerosene in your hip pocket. Chop it out.

"All that is left is sawing the back. The saw cut opens. The critical moment is at hand. Loosen spurs in the bark. If a tree splits it can crush a man to death. Have to be ready to move down and move down in a hurry.

"The top begins to go. Saw faster. Move around to the back side. 'Timber!' Mouth dry as sin, scalp tingling, feeling scared. Sawing for all you're worth. The trunk rearing back and then suddenly the top is off and sailing through space, crashing on the ground. Brace yourself to take the shock. A thrill shoots through you. Get ready to ride. The tree snaps back and you cut a wild arc across the sky. Whooping at the top of your lungs. Ride it out. Like a bucking bronc trying to throw you. Each buck not quite as strong as the one before it.

"Eventually the tree quits swaying. Ease your grip and the quiet floats around you. And then the rigging crew hollers up and wants to know if you're ready for the rigging. The magic of the moment is broken."

6

DAREDEVIL

The steepest and longest log flume in the world was the Sanger Flume. It ran from the heart of California's redwood country to the town of Sanger 54 miles away in the San Joaquin Valley. It dropped 4,300 feet in the first 13 miles.

In 1903 a daredevil journalist, Bailey Millard, announced he would ride the water-fed flume and write about his experience. As Bailey and a photographer climbed into a makeshift boat the company manager commented, "I wouldn't ride down that flume if you were to give me the company."

Bailey took a seat on a wooden cracker box and the flume hand shoved them off, offering the advice, "You'll want to hold on. She'll run like the milltails of hell."

Bailey later wrote of the experience, "The whizzing landscape fused into a long, filmy, biographic blur. I cannot time the swiftness of the Devil's Slide any more than a man riding a cyclone can ... we passed high, tragic cliffs on the edge of which the flume clung by a sort of miracle .... The speed increased and we swam dizzily out upon a terrible trestle, the spindling timbers of which, as seen from an oncoming curve, seemed the flimsiest of supports. We crossed one creek thirteen times, darting out upon the bridges unexpectedly from blind curves."

Bailey concluded the article of his thrilling experience in *Everybody's* magazine, writing, "The ride is such a bit of brisk living as sets the blood all a-tingle and gives one a taste of recklessness. To make such a voyage every day would in time fill even the commonest of men with the abandon of the gods."

BOTTLES

The summer of 1895 a logging crew captured a black bear cub and taught it to drink beer. They named the bear Bottles. Bottles grew from a cute cub to a full-sized bear and the men collared and chained him to a tree. Each day when they returned from work Bottles would be sitting on his haunches, head tilted back, jaws open wide, begging beer. The chief amusement in camp was to pour bottle after bottle of beer into the bear's gaping mouth; but, in time, Bottles began demanding more beer than the men were willing to part with.

One evening after Bottles had imbibed too much, he was loaded in a wagon and hauled to the White House Inn, a drinking establishment in the Willamette Valley. The manager agreed to give Bottles a home and for the first few weeks the bear with the drinking habit was good for business. The patrons took turns buying beer and pouring it down Bottles's throat.

Before long buying beer for Bottles became the preliminary to someone's wrestling the bear. Bottles took on all comers and won every match until late one night he was thrown by a working man with wrestling experience. Bottles lay on the ground making no attempt to rise, and in answer to the jeers of the crowd he fell into a deep sleep and began snoring.

After that embarrassing defeat Bottles turned mean and growled and snarled whenever anyone approached him with an open bottle of beer. That is why, when an Easterner passing through the country stopped at the Inn and admired the quality of the bear's fur, the manager sold the bear to him. The stranger killed Bottles and the hide of the beer-drinking bear became a rug.

GREAT LAKES LOGGING

Long before the white pine timber in the New England states had been high graded, restless lumberjacks began moving to the Great Lakes region. It was thought this forest, stretching from the tip of Lake Erie to the western tip of Lake Superior and beyond, would last forever. It lasted for less than fifty years.

During this half-century farmers were moving onto the plains by the thousands and they demanded boards and shingles to build houses, barns and fences. Railroaders were laying rails across the continent. They had to have millions of wooden ties and timbers for bridges and trestles. The Great Lakes region supplied their needs.

The federal government had more land and timber than it knew what to do with and sold land to lumbermen and speculators at the going rate of $1.25 an acre. The Great Lakes forest, composed mostly of white pine, was well watered with rivers and streams capable of floating logs.

In one area, along the Saginaw River, there were more than 100 sawmills and in 1882 they cut one billion feet of lumber and sawed up 300 million shingles. When the Saginaw timber played out the lumberjacks moved to Manistee, Cheboygan, Chippewa Falls or any other area that was opening up. The lumberjacks lived a wild and unshackled life. They roamed at will and there was always a job waiting in the next camp.

The heyday of Great Lakes logging was in the 1880s when more than 100,000 lumberjacks fell timber in such a frenzy that no counts were kept on how many billion board feet of lumber was shipped out of the woods. The America of that era was rich in natural resources.

AN ORDINARY DAY

Back at the turn of the century a logger wrote the following letter describing a typical day working in the woods:

"At 4 in the morning the iron-headed old boss sticks his mug in the bunkhouse door and yells, 'Daylight in the swamp,' and the truth of it is it will be two hours till daylight but the boss isn't to be argued with and we all roll out and get on our frozen boots and mukluks. We gang into the grub house and at 6 o'clock that same boss yells, 'All out for the woods.'

"By daylight we arrive at our picnic ground and log cedar out of the swamp. Along about noon the cook and his crew show up. We brush snow off a flat log and sit down to eat in weather which is mostly around zero....

"At 4 o'clock, which is about dark in the winter, the boss yells, 'All in.' We get back to camp about 5 o'clock, as we walk two or three miles, wash up and get into the grub house. That coffee sure goes good. It is so black you could paint a boiler with it. After grub we go back to the bunkhouse and thaw out our boots and take off our shirts and some of us, after lighting up our old corncobs or taking a fresh chew of plug, play cards, some play checkers, some swap lies....

"At 9 o'clock the geezer of a boss comes in and yells, 'Lights out,' and then someone blows out the lights of the two smoked-up lanterns and we all hit the hay to be ready to begin a bigger day tomorrow."

THE GREAT MIGRATION

Far ranging lumberjacks began telling stories to the loggers of the Great Lakes states that in the Pacific Northwest and northern California there was timber that beat anything they had ever seen: bigger and taller pine, something called Douglas fir that grew fifteen feet on the stump and stretched 300 feet tall, and redwoods so enormous they grew into the clouds.

One by one or in small groups the lumberjacks were drawn to the new timber out west. By the turn of the twentieth century this westward movement rivaled the era of covered wagon pioneers over the Oregon Trail.

The timber barons also turned their attention west after reports from their cruisers told of tremendous stands of virgin timber in northern California, Oregon, Washington, Idaho and Montana. They had to pay more for land, up to $6 an acre, but the trees were so thick and tall a healthy profit was assured.

Timber barons moving west included Weyerhaeuser, Whitney, Simpson, Polson, Peavey, Blodgett, Griggs, Hartley, Clough and partners like Smith-Powers, Clark-Wilson, Brooks-Scanlon, Shevlin-Hixon and Pope-Talbot. They purchased millions of acres of prime timberland, built sawmills, went to logging and turning out lumber.

In their wake the timber barons and lumberjacks left deserted camps and sawmills scattered from the East Coast to the Great Lakes states. They walked away not troubling themselves to remove mattresses from the bunks or take down the stovepipe. Machinery was left to rust. After all, there was better timber out west.

THE FLOOD

Joe Nealy and C. Rhoades spent the winter of 1896 logging up the Sandy River drainage. They fell the big fir trees with crosscut saws and rolled the logs to the water's edge, expecting a spring freshet would carry them downstream to the mill.

The day the big storm blew in off the Pacific Ocean more than 500 logs were strung up and down the river. Nealy and Rhoades continued cutting trees in the pouring rain. It rained and rained. A cold wind blew up the gorge and finally Nealy and Rhoades quit. It was dangerous to fall in weather like that.

The rain continued all that afternoon and through the night, pounding on the tent the two loggers shared. Wind moaned through the trees. The river, choked with runoff, began to roar.

At the first light of day the men were up checking the level of the river. It was on the rise, carrying down limbs and chunks of brush. Water lapped at the logs.

"If it keeps rainin', if the river keeps risin', we're in a world of trouble. We'll lose everything," Nealy told his partner.

Rhoades grunted and shook his head, "Looks that way."

The steady downpour never diminished and the river poured over its banks. The flood raised the level of the Sandy River eleven feet in 24 hours and it swept away every last one of the 500 logs.

DEATH OF A LOGGER

Ed Tice was a logger back in the days when the woods resounded to the sharp crack of swinging axes, the muted swish of misery whips and earth-shattering crashes as 200-foot fir trees crashed to the ground.

One day the logging crew was working above Stillwater Creek, a trickle of water dripping over mossy rocks. Sunlight slanted between the big trees and fell in a dappled pattern on the lush, fern-covered forest floor. Ed finished bucking a log into 32-foot lengths and took a breather, watching a team of fallers work to drop another tree. They threw coal oil on the saw and with the rhythm of a fiddler's bow, they made music with the misery whip, drawing it back and forth. Every so often they stopped to tap the wedges, keeping the kerf open so the saw did not bind.

And then the kerf began to open on its own. The wood hinge creaked and groaned. "Timber!" the fallers hollered as they ran.

Ed watched the tree top wiggle and start slowly on the long arc that would bring it to the ground. He was beyond the reach of the tree, safe and out of danger.

The fallers watched as the big tree picked up speed and slammed into the underbrush amid a shower of snapping branches. The ground shook like an earthquake and a cloud of dust and duff was kicked into the sunlight.

And then there was a second crash. The falling tree had caused a nearby snag to give way. It fell, striking Ed where he sat.

That afternoon the logging crew buried Ed there above Stillwater Creek. They left a patch of virgin timber in the heart of the forest to mark his grave.

FIRE SEASON

The drought of 1910 was to blame for one of the worst fire seasons on record.

Nearly every day that summer dark storm clouds rolled over the horizon, but instead of spilling raindrops the clouds hurled thunderbolts into the parched woods. By mid-July there were more than 3,000 fires burning out of control in the Pacific Northwest. Loggers and rangers from the fledgling U.S. Forest Service could not stop the inferno. President Taft ordered ten companies of soldiers into the woods and to a man they prayed the winds would stay calm and the rains would come soon.

On August 20 a mighty wind blew in off the Pacific. One forest ranger on a fire line in Northern Idaho reported the 70 mile per hour wind "sounded like the roar of 1,000 freight trains passing over that many trestles."

The gale blew for two full days and in that time more than 3 million acres of prime timberland went up in smoke. Men caught in crown fires ran side by side with animals fleeing the holocaust. Many men survived by laying in creeks with water-soaked blankets pulled over them. Others escaped to mining tunnels or burrowed into rock slides.

The experienced woodsmen, for the most part, kept their heads but some of the temporaries, drafted to work on the fire lines from the bars and back alleys, tried to out-run the firewall. One man shot himself rather than be burned to death. In all 85 fire fighters lost their lives.

A great cloud of smoke covered the region from the Pacific Ocean to the Great Plains. When the cloud hit Denver the temperature dropped 19 degrees in 10 minutes and in Cheyenne, Wyoming it was dark as night in the middle of the day and the temperature skidded to 38 degrees.

On August 23 the wind died and rain began to fall. The fire season of 1910 was over.

LOGGERS' JARGON

Johnny Bedore was a rawboned, redheaded Irishman, a tramp logger who drifted into Klamath County back in the '20s. He normally worked in the vast ponderosa forests twelve hours a day, six days a week, and lived in logging camps where the night air was cut by the strong smell of socks and longjohns steaming behind the bunkhouse stove.

One day Johnny was loading a flatcar at the landing when an accident occurred. A mishandled log swung around and knocked him off the top of the load. He tried to get up but could not. One leg was obviously broken and from the pain in his side, he knew he had cracked or broken several ribs.

Johnny was taken to the hospital in Klamath Falls. A nurse came around to his room with a handful of compensation papers to fill out. She wrote his name, date of birth, and employer. The next question asked the patient to describe the accident.

"In your own words, Mr. Bedore, will you tell me how the accident happened?" she requested.

Johnny, who had lived around logging camps all his life, began, "Well, Miss, it's 'bout like this. See, I'm a top loader by trade. Experienced. Today the squirrel we had on the ground running the show was green as grass. We had a long, slippery school marm on the landing and I signaled the puncher to give the St. John's flip but he up and gave her the Cannuck instead. The jammer cocked her tail and she saginawed, knocked me off the top, breakin' my leg and three of my slats."

The girl, with a puzzled look on her face, stated, "Mr. Bedore, I am afraid I do not understand."

Johnny replied, "Me, either, Miss. How could a man pull a Cannuck when you call for a St. John's flip? Mystery to me."

THE FIRST WESTERN LOGGERS

The men of the Pacific Fur Company were the first Americans to log west of the Mississippi. They arrived at the mouth of the Columbia River in the spring of 1811 and began clearing land for a trading post (Fort Astoria).

Alexander Ross, a company clerk, wrote, "The place selected for the emporium of the West was studded with gigantic trees of almost incredible size, many measured fifty feet in girth....

"After viewing the height and breadth of the tree to be cut down, the party, with some labor, would erect a scaffold round it; this done, four men -- for that was the number appointed to each of those huge trees -- would then mount the scaffold, and commence cutting.... Sometimes it required two days or more to fall one tree.

"There is an art in falling a tree but unfortunately none of us had learned that art, and hours together would be spent in conjectures and discussions; one calling out that it would fall here, another, there ... and at last, when all hands were assembled to witness the fall, how often were we disappointed! The tree would still stand erect, bidding defiance to our efforts, while every now and then some of the most impatient or foolhardy would venture to jump on the scaffold and give a blow or two more. Much time was spent in this manner before the mighty tree gave way, but it seldom came to the ground. So thick was the forest, and so close the trees together, that in its fall it would often rest its ponderous top on some other friendly tree ... and when we finally did succeed in falling a tree both stump and tree had to be blown to pieces by gunpowder before either could be removed.

"Nearly two months of this laborious and incessant toil passed, and we had scarcely yet an acre of ground cleared. In the meantime two of our men were wounded by the falling of trees, one had his hand blown off by gunpowder and three were killed by natives."

HIGH CLIMBER AGAIN

Fred Noah was born in a logging camp and by the time he was eighteen years old he was high climbing. Even at that young age he was considered one of the best and fastest climbers in the Northwest.

One day Fred topped a tree, making a 134-foot spar pole, just before the noon whistle sounded. He planned to eat a leisurely lunch and finish his work, but the boss came around and asked him to cut his lunch short. He wanted Fred to go up, hang the block and make the guylines fast so they could rig the spar. He said he wanted to be yarding logs by the middle of the afternoon.

The sun was directly overhead. High climbers do not like to climb into the sun because it blinds them, but Fred made an exception. He adjusted his spurs, flipped his safety rope around the tree and started climbing. The loggers ate their lunches and watched.

Near the 130-foot mark Fred paused. Squinting into the sun he misjudged the distance to the top of the spar pole, took two quick steps up, flipped the rope. It came up and over. Fred's surprised holler reached the horrified men an instant after they realized he was falling.

Instinctively, Fred curled himself into a tight ball. He hit the ground on his knees, elbows and forehead, landing on a steep sidehill between a stump and a log. The impact shoved his hip bones out of their sockets, shattered elbows, arms and shoulders, broke ribs and collar bones and knocked a silver dollar-sized hole in his skull.

The men rushed to him. They tied shirts and jackets together to fashion a stretcher and carried Fred to the landing. He was rushed to the hospital where a team of doctors worked around the clock to save his life.

Two years after the accident Fred limped to a tree, threw his safety rope around the trunk and, digging spurs into the bark, he started up. He had made it back. He was a high climber again.

19

SURVIVOR

On March 9, 1936 Paul Kusturin was run over by a train.

At the time Paul was working day shift as brakeman for the Long-Bell Lumber Company, riding the engine as it backed down a long grade pulling 35 empty cars coupled to the front of the engine. As they approached a siding he climbed over the end of the tender and descended the ladder. He planned to step off the moving train, hurry ahead and throw the switch. But he lost his balance and fell between the rails.

Paul had a fraction of a second to choose between attempting to throw himself from the track, realizing if he did he would be cut in half by the fast approaching wheels, or staying where he was and being ground beneath the locomotive. He turned his head to the side and tried to flatten himself as much as possible.

The engine reached him and instinctively he grabbed the axle. The engineer, Charlie Dunn, heard blood-curdling screams, threw the brake and 190 feet later the train shrieked to a stop.

Charlie and the fireman, Pat Murphy, located Paul. It was impossible to move the engine in either direction without hurting him more so they used brute strength to pull him, crying out in pain, from the machinery.

Throughout the ordeal Paul never lost consciousness. He was bleeding, had several broken ribs, a broken left leg, dislocated right leg, a severe concussion and spinal injuries. He was rushed to a first aid station where they kept him for six hours waiting for him to die.

When it looked as if he might live, an ambulance was dispatched and transported the injured man 30 miles to Longview Memorial hospital. Paul was hospitalized several months and spent more time at home convalescing. But within a year of the accident he had recovered and returned to work on the railroad.

LOGGING THE REDWOODS

The first loggers in the redwood forests of the Pacific coast were disgruntled miners who had failed to strike it rich.

The woods boss (bull buck) assigned two men (choppers) to fall each giant tree. Their equipment included a plumb bob for determining the lean of the tree, double-edged axes, several saws varying in length from eight to twelve feet, wedges and sledge hammers. They would work on a scaffolding usually eight to ten feet above the ground where the trunk narrowed above its bole.

From the scaffolding the choppers made an undercut on the side the tree would fall. Other men cleaned a bed to receive the tree. When the undercut was completed the choppers moved to the opposite side and began chopping and cutting. They used wedges to keep the great bulk of the tree from settling back and closing the cut. It often took a week of hard work to fall a single redwood.

Once a tree was cut buckers cut it into logs and peelers pried off the thick, shaggy bark. Teams of oxen, up to sixteen yoked in pairs, were used to haul the logs over skidroads. The low sections of road were paved with smaller logs laid crosswise. To make the pull easier, water boys ran behind the oxen to dampen the skids.

At first logging was confined to coastal areas where rivers could be used as waterways for carrying logs to the mill. Floating logs were held in log jams until fall rains came. On smaller rivers check dams were constructed and when there was enough water the dam would be blown and the logs would shoot downstream in man-made floods. Coastal sawmills cut the logs into lumber which was shipped to San Francisco and sold for up to $75 per thousand board feet.

With the invention of the steam donkey in 1881 the face of the redwood forests was forever changed. Steam was used to power saws and to yard the logs to a landing. Railroad spur lines were built into the woods. Within a few short generations the vast redwood forests had been subdued.

PEAVEY

One warm spring day in 1855 Joe Peavey of Bangor, Maine wandered away from his blacksmith shop to the covered bridge across the Penobscot River. He lay on his stomach and through a crack in the floor watched a crew of lumberjacks attempting to break a log jam.

The lumberjacks were having a devil of a time because the tools they were using, called swing dogs, were awkward to use. While Joe watched he was suddenly struck with an idea for a simple but efficient tool to move logs. He ran back to his blacksmith shop where, with his son Daniel, he worked to fashion the tool that had come to him in the vision.

They took a stout staff of ash wood and encircled it near one end with an iron collar. A free-swinging hook with a sharp spike was fastened into a slot in this collar. It allowed the collar and iron hook to move up and down but not sideways.

In addition to being awkward the swing dogs were also extremely dangerous and could throw a man over a log when he put his shoulder into it. The peavey, as it was to be called, was such a tremendous improvement that as soon as a lumberjack used one he would throw away his swing dog.

Today lumberjacks around the world continue to use the tool that came to Joe Peavey in a vision, the simple tool that erased some of the back-breaking work of rolling logs and saved many loggers' lives.

REDWOOD OBSERVATORY

For the 1893 Columbian Exposition in Chicago, the United States government came up with the grand idea of a unique display. They would have an observatory carved from the trunk of a California redwood.

The tree selected was a giant sequoia growing just outside the boundary of the newly created Sequoia National Park. It was estimated to be 3,000 years old and measured 300 feet tall. It took 18 workers linking hands to reach all the way around the massive 90-foot base. They posed for a picture and then went to work building a scaffolding up to the 50-foot mark. They managed to fall the top 250 feet but as it started down it kicked back, smashing the scaffolding and forcing the fallers to jump.

The top 14 feet of the 50-foot stump was hollowed out, leaving a shell of two feet of bark and six inches of wood. This was cut into staves. The staves were numbered and crated for shipment out of the woods by mule team. The next two feet was cut as a block. Another 14 feet of shell was taken and cut into staves. This left a 20-foot stump, looking both magnificent and pathetic, that was afterward referred to as the "Chicago Stump" by the locals.

The parts were transported by rail to Chicago and reassembled into a roofed observation tower. Visitors to the exhibit were allowed to climb a 30-foot spiral staircase inside the stump that passed midway through a hole in the solid section. The reason for the solid landing was to prove to any skeptics that the stump had once been a real tree.

After the Chicago fair the redwood observation tower was taken to the Mall in Washington, D.C., where it remained for several years until it was disassembled for storage. Where it was stored is unknown. The government lost it.

LOGGING CAMP

Two young men, Lee Terry and David Denny, came west with their families in 1851. Their fathers and mothers, brothers and sisters and aunts and uncles stayed at Fort Vancouver while the two headed north over the Cowlitz Trail in search of a site to establish a logging camp.

They settled on tree-covered Alki Point in Puget Sound and with an ax and hammer, the only tools they had, they went to work falling trees and building a cabin. Word was sent to their families instructing them to take passage on the first available ship.

It took the families a week to float down the Columbia River and sail up the stormy coast. The ship was overcrowded and everyone was seasick.

Lee was alone that day when he heard the rattle of the anchor and looked up and saw the ship. He raced down to the beach, cupped his hands around his mouth and hollered, "Welcome to your new home."

The date was November 13 and the rainy season had begun. The sky was colored dismal gray and a swirling wind blew the mist around. Fog hid the long line of the Olympic Mountains which were so glorious on a clear day. And as the families, numbering 12 adults and 12 children, were rowed to shore they could see the little cabin protruding from the deep forest. There was no front door. The roof was unfinished.

While the men moved the supplies and baggage from the beach, where an incoming tide threatened to wash it away, the ship set sail and disappeared into the fog.

Several of the women, homesick, lonely and cold, sat on a log and cried. This was not what they had expected when their husbands had coaxed them into coming west to set up a logging camp.

WOMANLESS WEST

The early-day logging camps were conspicuously short of women. In 1860 it was estimated that west of the Rocky Mountains there were ten men for every woman and that in most cases the woman was a pioneer wife who had crossed the plains with her husband and family.

Asa Mercer, a 22-year-old resident of Puget Sound, offered to do something for the local loggers. He traveled to the East Coast and persuaded eleven young women to come west with him. They traveled by ship to the Isthmus of Panama, crossed over and caught a steamer north. The ladies arrived in Seattle to a jubilant welcome on May 16, 1864. They were quickly courted and whisked to the altar by eleven lucky men.

This success prompted Mercer to plan a second, more ambitious undertaking. He collected a $300 fee from single loggers as down payments on brides, promising them he would use his friendship -- which dated back to his boyhood in Illinois -- with President Abraham Lincoln to help import 500 Eastern maidens.

Mercer traveled to Washington, D.C., but before he could meet with Lincoln the president was assassinated. Others were unsympathetic to Mercer's proposal and one New York newspaper frightened away hundreds of prospects by branding Mercer a white slave trader. Mercer spent a year on the East Coast and was able to talk only 46 young women into accompanying him.

They arrived in Seattle the night of May 23, 1866 and, even though there were not enough young women to satisfy all the investors, Mercer was able to explain the problems he had encountered and vindicate himself. According to one report the meeting closed "with the best of good will towards Mr. Mercer and all concerned."

Mercer took one of the young women, Annie Stephens, as his bride, moved to Wyoming and became a successful rancher.

THE WOBBLIES

The Industrial Workers of the World, known as the I.W.W. or the "Wobblies", was organized in 1905 by Big Bill Haywood, a huge one-eyed miner from Salt Lake City. His goal was to unite all working stiffs.

Wobbly halls opened in Portland, Seattle, Tacoma and Spokane and organizational drives were made to unionize loggers and sawmill workers. By 1907 the Wobblies were flexing their muscles. Big Bill called for a sawmill strike in Portland unless mill owners doubled the wages, to $3 a day, and agreed to an eight-hour shift, down from eleven hours. All but one of the large sawmills were forced to close. But in the end the strike was broken when police threw strike leaders in jail on charges ranging from disorderly conduct to attempted arson.

For a decade the Wobblies kept the timber industry of the Pacific Northwest in a state of turmoil. The most celebrated Wobbly demonstration occurred on November 5, 1916. Denied the right to exercise free speech in Everett, Washington, the Wobblies chartered the *Verona* in Seattle and packed her with 400 determined activists. When the ship docked in Everett a gun battle ensued. The smoke cleared, seven men were dead and 68 lay wounded. After a lengthy trial the court determined that no one was guilty.

A year later the Wobblies staged the largest strike in logging and sawmill history. They shut down 85% of the camps and mills in the Pacific Northwest. The few operators who did run were sabotaged with mysterious mill fires, spikes driven into logs and derailed logging trains.

The strike was broken when the federal government intervened. Lumber was needed for the war effort. Big Bill Haywood instructed his members to return to work but to continue sabotaging their employers.

The government prevailed. Big Bill fled to Russia and Wobbly organizers were sent to prison where they remained until 1923 when President Harding pardoned them.

TRAIN DISASTER

One of the worst railroad wrecks in logging history occurred in Coos County, Oregon on November 25, 1912.

That fateful morning dawned cold and rainy. A weather front blew in off the Pacific and the hills were draped in fog. At the Seeley & Anderson camp a Shay locomotive departed on its inaugural run of a new four-mile link between camp and the Coquille River. It pulled three loaded log cars and carried three crewmen and four passengers, including two injured loggers going out to the doctor.

The train approached a canyon spanned by a wooden trestle 100 feet high and 500 feet long. The engineer, thinking they were going a little too fast, applied the brakes. A forward strain was put on the trestle. Above the noise of the locomotive a throaty groan and a high-pitched creaking were audible. Then the trestle began to sway, slowly at first but quickly becoming violent. The engineer let up on the brake but it had no noticeable effect on the quaking trestle.

"Boys, we're gone!" shouted the engineer and the first girder buckled. It was like dominos after that with girder after girder falling over. The trestle came apart and tumbled into the canyon, carrying the train with it.

The Shay locomotive landed upside-down. Scalding steam spewed from its boilers onto the men inside the cab. One man was able to pull himself free, climb from the debris and hike back to camp.

Rescuers picked their way through the twisted girders and after 24 hours they freed the last man. Their efforts proved futile. Three men had been killed outright and three others, trapped in the wreckage and scalded by steam, died within a few hours of their rescue. Only one man survived.

DOLBEER'S DONKEY

John Dolbeer came west in the gold rush of 1850. After a few months of searching for gold he found greater potential for wealth in supplying the miners with lumber. He and a partner began a logging and sawmill operation in the redwood country of northern California.

John's contribution to the partnership was his ability to engineer machinery and problem-solving devices. Forever looking for ways to streamline the operation, he invented a high-speed, circular saw that replaced the slow up-and-down gang saw. A band saw, an endless steel belt with razor-sharp teeth capable of cutting at a high speed with minimal waste, superseded the circular saw.

Until 1881 oxen and horses dragged logs over skidroads; but in that year John's grandest invention replaced the animals. It was a small steam engine, called a donkey, that powered a capstan-like drum that reeled in logs to a landing.

The original invention was improved by replacing manila rope with wire cable, adding more drums, and increasing the size of the engine. By the turn of the century every logging operation of any size was switching to Dolbeer's donkey. It remained popular until the 1930s when the internal combustion engine made the donkey obsolete.

THE WHISTLE

The earliest sawmill in the Far West began operating in 1827 near Fort Vancouver on the Columbia River. Over the next several decades other mills, also operated by water power, began sawing logs. Commercial logging and sawmilling did not begin until after gold was discovered at Sutter's Mill in California in 1848 and lumber for use in the mines was suddenly in great demand.

Water-powered sawmills were slow and dependent on a steady source of water so in 1849 two Eastern businessmen, W.P. Abrams and Cyrus Reed, brought a steam-operated saw around the Horn to Portland, Oregon. They established their sawmill on the west bank of the Willamette River, upriver from a large Indian camp.

The day the boiler was fired and the first log was locked onto the carriage the Indians, dressed in beads and their finest buckskins, gathered around. They watched smoke belching from the stack and steam escape from the safety valve. They were not prepared for the lumberman's tradition of starting the work shift with a blast from the steam whistle.

The whistle screamed and the Indians ran away into the woods. It was several days before they had the courage to return to the site and watch the steam-operated saw cut the big fir logs into boards.

LOG RAFT

At the age of fifteen Simon Benson immigrated from Norway to the United States. He worked a dozen years as a lumberjack in Wisconsin before coming to the Northwest and going to work in a logging camp at $40 a month. He was frugal and saved enough to buy six oxen and set himself up as an independent bullwacker.

Profits from bullwacking were plowed into timberland and by 1900 Benson operated a far-flung logging enterprise including a sawmill, a logging railroad and 15 logging camps. He calculated his profits at nearly $3,000 a day.

Adding to his empire Benson built a large sawmill in San Diego to serve the growing lumber needs of Southern California. Soon he discovered that shipping Northwest logs in ocean-going vessels ate up most of the profits. The cost of rail shipment was also prohibitive. Benson decided to try rafting logs.

Rafting logs had been attempted on both coasts but failed when heavy seas broke loose the logs. Benson invented a cigar-shaped cradle to give the log raft a rigid and streamlined form.

In the quiet of Wallace Slough on the lower Columbia River, the cradle was filled with logs by a floating derrick. The cradle gradually sank into the water. When one and one-half million board feet were loaded, a heavy anchor chain was stretched from stem to stern to serve as a backbone for the raft. Another million and a half board feet of logs were loaded on top and wrapped with 175 tons of chains.

The first raft, pulled by a powerful tug, made the 1,100 mile journey to San Diego in 20 days without losing a single log. It was followed by many more rafts, some of them 1,000 feet in length, drawing 28 feet of water and carrying 6 million board feet. The rafts provided Benson's mill with an endless supply of logs, made him a multi-millionaire and opened the practice of transporting logs on the high seas.

CLEARING LAND

In pioneer days the mammoth trees of the Far West were considered adversaries that had to be cleared from the land so it could be farmed.

The protected valleys west of the Cascade mountain range were covered with Douglas fir trees fifteen feet in diameter and reaching 300 feet up into the clouds. A man with an ax or a saw could not hope to make much of a dent in the forest. The most popular means of downing timber was to drill into the stump, build fires in the bore holes and wait for the fire to burn through. Eventually the tree would collapse under its own weight.

During the winter of 1892 homesteader Branch Tucker worked to make a clearing in the forest. He tapped several dozen fir trees and early one morning set fires in the bore holes. He nursed the fires all day; late in the afternoon a wind came up and the trees began to topple.

Finally only one stubborn tree was standing. It refused to fall. Branch went to the cabin where his wife fixed him supper. As he ate he listened, anticipating the crash as the tree fell.

After supper Branch lit a lantern. His young son wanted to know, "Where are you going, Daddy?"

"Out to check that last tree, make sure the fire's still going. Want to come along?" asked Branch.

Branch and the boy walked into the night, the lantern giving off a circle of yellow light around them. The wind had died. A light, misty rain was beginning to fall.

They cautiously approached the tree. Suddenly there was a sharp cracking sound. The tree was going over. Branch held the lantern over his head quickly trying to determine which way the tree was falling. He grabbed his son roughly and shoved him out of harm's way.

There was a tremendous crash and the light went out. The boy called into the dark, "Daddy, are you all right?" But there was no answer. His father was dead.

SKIDROAD

The skidroad was the Western loggers' greatest contribution to moving logs from the woods to the mill.

Back in the Great Lakes states logs were skidded over the frozen ground on sleighs or under high wheels. West of the Rockies winters are warmer and snow rarely lasts. The ground is too muddy and too rough for high wheels. Faced with these conditions the inventive lumberjacks developed the skidroad.

Henry Yesler is credited with building the first skidroad from the woods to his mill on Puget Sound in 1852. After it was no longer used for skidding logs it became the main street of the growing settlement of Seattle.

Skidroads were built by first clearing a path in the forest and then placing logs crossways on the path, partially buried in the soft ground. They were like ties on a railroad and allowed logs to be skidded over the top without hanging up on rocks or becoming mired in the mud. Teams of oxen or work horses could pull long turns of logs over a skidroad.

The skidroad was the center stage of any logging show. In later years the term was used to define the street in any West Coast city where loggers hung out when they came to civilization. It was a tough place. Loggers called it Skid Road and were proud of the name.

One logger, Walter McCulloch, stated, "Careless reporters with dirt in their ears have written the name Skid Road wrong and have referred to it as skid row so often that this miserable, phony term is accepted by the ignorant. There's no such damn thing and there never was. The street of saloons, card rooms, flop houses and sporting houses is Skid Road. Let's hear no more about skid row."

BAD LUCK BUNCH

"I'm edgy as a rabbit in a coyote den," remarked one of the loggers at McLaughlin's Camp at Black Rock. "Three years. No accidents."

"Got to be a record," stated another. "Men been killed all around us. Lucky. That's all there is to it."

"I got this gut feelin' Lady Luck is 'bout to turn her back on us," the first logger interjected. "You know our turn is comin'. Someone in this camp's gonna have an accident. I can't take the suspense no more. I'm drawing my pay, movin' on."

In the morning the logger departed camp. That day the remarkable string of three years without an accident in McLaughlin's Camp continued. But the following afternoon donkey engineer Rainous Russell narrowly escaped death when a log came loose and rolled down the hill. He jumped clear but the choker hit him in the face, giving him a pair of black eyes and a terrible headache.

Three days later Frank Colgra, a timber faller, was chopping out the undercut when a freak wind toppled the tree he was working on, pinning him under it. The crew worked to tunnel under the tree and free Frank but he died before they could get him out.

The floodgate of pent-up accidents broke loose: a cable came loose from the high lead and whipped around the body of a choker setter like a coiled snake, breaking several ribs; a man stepped in a hole and twisted an ankle; one of the buckers nearly chopped off his foot with his ax.

All the accidents occurred in a ten-day period in October 1909. Loggers in surrounding camps began referring to the boys working for McLaughlin as the "Bad Luck Bunch".

SILENT WOOD

Back in the days of steam logging the entry level job in the woods was whistle punk. Usually a boy or young man was hired as whistle punk and he was responsible for communicating between the choker setters and the donkey engineer. On his signal the cable line, with logs attached, was reeled in to the landing.

A logging outfit working in the woods of Puget Sound hired a sixteen-year-old boy named Ed to be whistle punk. The men liked Ed. They joked with him and gave him a hard time because that was what loggers did with a new whistle punk. It was part of the initiation process.

One afternoon after only a few days on the job, a terrible accident involved the boy. Lumberjack Torger Birkelann recalled that fateful afternoon, "We were hard at work when all of a sudden everything seemed to stop. No whistles. No sound in the woods. Silence. I knew right away something bad had happened and sure enough before long I saw a group of men come walking my way, walking real slow, carrying something between them. I walked up to meet them.

"They had Ed. Tenderly they laid him down. There was nothing could be done for the boy. He was unconscious. At least he wasn't sufferin' none. There was no doctor within reach and not much could have been done if there had been. The men said he signaled and the main line hung up and then came free. It caught Ed and hurled him into the brush. His back was broke sure as if two strong men had pulled a wish bone apart. Terrible. Terrible.

"And while we waited for the Lord to take Ed to the Great Beyond all of us rough-appearing loggers let the tears run unashamedly down our cheeks. Ah, it was a truly sad day. All you could do was shake your head and say, 'He was just a boy. Just a boy with his whole life in front of him.'

"We never went back to work that day. No one felt like working."

SKID ROAD

Every logging town of any size had a Skid Road where working men gathered to brawl, booze and womanize.

In Seattle, entrepreneur John Considine came up with an idea to combine a saloon, theater and bawdy house under one roof. For the opening of his People's Theater he imported Little Egypt from New York where the celebrated dancer had been jailed briefly for dancing in the nude. The People's Theatre was an overwhelming success. The owner made so much money that eventually he went legitimate and took his theatre on the road as the nation's first traveling vaudeville show.

Seattle's most famous house-of-ill-repute was a place operated by flamboyant Lou Graham. In 1889 she built a four-story brick palace and struck a deal with local government officials; in return for police not raiding her establishment she would contribute a license fee of $50 per month per gaming table and $10 per month per girl in her employ to the municipal fund. As an added inducement, she promised all city officials visiting her house would be treated as guests, without charge.

Lou had a novel way of promoting her business. Every Sunday she would have her best-looking girls dress in colorful finery and ride through the business district in surreys. In 1903 Seattle's most famous madam died. In her will Lou left the bulk of her fortune, one quarter million dollars, to the county school system.

RUNNING CHUTE

John Cook, a logger from Michigan, came west in the late 1800s. He purchased a large tract of virgin sugar pine timber in the Siskiyou Mountains near the Oregon/California border.

Men immediately went to work falling the timber but Cook had a problem. How would he get the logs from the mountains to his mill built along the Klamath River 3,000 feet below? His solution was to build a running chute, a steep trough of hand-hewn timbers.

Cook's chute dropped over the edge and came straight down the wall of the Klamath River canyon, through a cut blasted in a rock outcropping, across a slight depression on a trestle, through a second cut, and ended at a huge mill pond fed by the Klamath River. The sides and bottom of the steep trough were smoothed and greased.

Cook timed the first log sent down the chute and boasted that the trip took only 22 1/2 seconds, with the average speed being 90 miles an hour. It arrived smoking from the friction. When it hit the water it made a tremendous splash and floated to the surface sizzling and steaming.

The running chute and mill were operated profitably for a decade. In 1902 a fire destroyed the sawmill and the small town of Klamathon. By then the majority of the timber had been logged and Cook elected not to rebuild.

All that remains of one of the most famous running chutes is a thin scar on the steep wall of the Klamath River canyon.

SECOND TREE

Philip Grabinski once held the Northwest spar tree climbing record, scaling a 150-foot spar tree in 63 seconds and taking 18 seconds more to drop to the ground.

He wrote of his high climbing experiences, "First tree I topped was at North Bend, Washington and I was scared just enough to be very careful. I started up this tree which was about five feet through, so it took about 22 feet of rope to go around the tree and my body. The tree was 180 feet high and 18 inches through on top, so it took about nine feet of rope up there. When I got ready to top I took a good look around. I wanted to know where I'd be after the top started over and as soon as I saw all that spare rope that I had taken in as I went up the tree, I took it and threw it around the tree again. Having two ropes around me I felt much better.

"When I topped this tree it fell and didn't even give me a thrill. I thought this business was pretty easy until I topped the second tree. It was much larger and as I was chopping, my body was swinging on the long, sharp spurs. They kept working steadily deeper into the tree and pretty soon the top cracked and instead of going away from me as I had figured, it came right at me. When I tried to get around the tree I found my spurs so deep I couldn't get them out and right then and there I started thinking of many things, mostly about what a bad boy I had been.

"It was a heavy top and as it came over it pulled the whole trunk of the tree with it until the top was about 45 degrees, then it broke loose and the tree swung back with me. The top fell straight down and cleared me plenty, so now I know it is impossible to get hit with the top of a tree up there. Yep, that was my second tree."

OXEN AND THE TOP HAT

An Eastern gentleman came west in the late 1800s, filed on a timber claim and went to work falling the big cedar trees and splitting them into shakes.

He worked all that first winter and come spring he hiked to the neighbor's and asked if he could hire the neighbor to haul shingles to town.

"I'm busy as all get-out," claimed the neighbor. "But I ain't usin' the oxen or the wagon. Take 'em."

The Easterner was wary of the big lumbering animals but he loaded the wagon and started to town. The oxen seemed to be on their best behavior and waited patiently while he sold and unloaded the shakes. With money in his pocket and a new top hat on his head, the Easterner led the oxen toward home.

Coming up the long grade out of town the oxen became excited, throwing their heads and breaking into a lumbering trot. The Easterner attempted to hold them back. When he could not, he jumped in the wagon and pulled on the brake. By then the oxen were running over the summit and down the other side.

Many times during that wild ride the Easterner thought of abandoning the jostling wagon but it was moving too fast to make a safe exit. At last the oxen came to an abrupt stop on their own. The Easterner looked around and realized they were in his neighbor's barnyard.

He climbed off the wagon, took inventory and discovered the only damage was the loss of his top hat. When the neighbor offered his team and wagon again, the Easterner lied, said he had made arrangements to have the remainder of his shingles hauled to town.

LOG PIRATES

Under cover of darkness log pirates, individuals or small gangs, often sneaked in and stole a few logs out of the log booms lining the major rivers of the West. The logs were sold to operators of bootleg sawmills who never questioned the ownership of logs brought to them.

In the summer of 1920 a group of log pirates pulled off the largest theft in the history of logging. It occurred on the Fraser River of British Columbia and involved a huge raft of No. 1 Douglas fir logs destined for a Puget Sound sawmill. The logs were tied in a cove and a good-natured fellow named Halstrom was guarding them.

Late one afternoon a tugboat approached Halstrom's floating guard shack, gave a couple friendly toots and the captain called out, "Hello. Is my raft ready to go?" Halstrom noted the name of the tug was the *Daisy Ann* and that its home port was Seattle. He assumed it had been sent from the Puget Sound sawmill and had come for the logs.

The *Daisy Ann* eased up to the shack and the captain and three-man crew tied off and joined Halstrom. The captain produced a jug of whiskey. It made the rounds as the men discussed such far-ranging topics as the weather and the state of national politics. They swapped logging stories and told about floods they had survived and accidents they had witnessed. They talked, drank and over the course of several hours became best friends.

It was after dark when the captain announced they had to be on their way. The jug was left with Halstrom while the crew of the *Daisy Ann* worked to free the log raft and pull it into the current of the Fraser.

The following morning Halstrom was rousted from a deep sleep by another tugboat. The crew claimed they had come for the big log raft. But the cove was bare. More than one million board feet of No. 1 Douglas fir logs had disappeared and were never recovered.

HUMBOLDT

One Skid Road drinking establishment operated for the benefit of the logger was Big Fred Hewett's Humboldt Saloon in Aberdeen, Washington.

Newspaper man James Stevens wrote, "The Humboldt was a place for honest drinking and performing; a logger's life was perfectly safe inside its doors. In the Humboldt no gambler could bilk him out of his hard-made earnings. No painted dancer could spill chloral in his whiskey glass. No tin-eared plug-ugly could sock him behind the ear and then frisk his pockets. If the logger himself began to yearn for battle he found himself bouncing over the sidewalk outside, with Big Fred's voice roaring behind him, 'Come back when you want to be decent! I do all the fightin' for this place!'

"The old-time loggers knew the Humboldt as a trusty bank. When they flooded in from the woods before the Fourth of July and Christmas the big safe often held as much as $20,000, the deposits of loggers who wanted to protect themselves from the cutthroats and harpies. Each man's money was put in a separate envelope. His name and sum were marked down until the whole sum was gone. In one year the Humboldt cashed $600,000 worth of checks.

"When the logger got work-hungry, Big Fred supplied him with a bottle to carry back to the woods to 'sober up on' before he took to the ax and saw again."

CHANGED MAN

Ted Goodwin was a preacher who traveled to the many Northwest logging camps to speak the word of God.

In later years Ted received a letter from a logger who described himself in his younger days as "so tough that given the opportunity I would rather fight than sit down to a home-cooked meal." The logger went on to remind Ted of an incident that occurred in the coast range of Washington in 1934.

"Ted, do you recall the time, out in the woods, the time I was a-fighting a big butt log in bad hang-up?" the man wanted to know. "I was in mud up to my knees, down in a cut, trying to pull slack in the choker and roll the hook under the log. I lost my temper. Said some words that are unprintable. Said a lot of words that are unprintable. In fact, I hate to admit it, but I cursed like an ordinary sailor.

"All at once I got some slack in the choker, rolled the hook under the log, set it and stepped back. I was shaking the mud off my gloves as I walked round the end of that big log and there you were. I never been so embarrassed in my whole life. I was ashamed of what I had said, all those terrible, terrible words. Ashamed my temper had got the best of me.

"I want to set the record straight. I went on to become an all around rigging man and extra loader. It's been almost forty years since I last saw you. I'm writing this letter to let you know that coming face-to-face with you that day, like that, made a changed man out of me. Just thought you ought to know, Ted."

45

BORN LOGGER

Tom spent his life roaming west of the Rocky Mountains as a hunter and free trapper. In his later years he settled down in Oregon, built a log cabin and cleared ground to farm.

He spent several years in the valley before pioneers drifted in to claim homestead ground. One of the early emigrants was a young man, James Neall, who visited Tom and asked, "Any jobs you might have where I could earn money?"

"There ain't no money in Oregon," drawled Tom. "The standard of exchange in these parts is salmon or wheat."

He thought for a moment and continued, "I do have a job needs to be done. See that oak tree uprooted there by the corner of my cabin? I need to have it worked up. I'll pay ya five bushels of wheat."

"I'll do it," offered James. "When can I start?"

"I was fixin' to head to the settlement 'fore daylight," said Tom. "Be gone overnight. If ya want to start tomorrow, suits me fine."

The next morning James attacked the tree with an ax and after several hours of diligent work managed to sever the roots. He switched to a bore and sunk a number of holes into the hard wood. He filled the holes with powder and set off an explosion that blew the tree apart. And then he gathered the fragments of wood into a pile and set fire to them.

Late in the afternoon of the following day Tom arrived home. All that remained of the big oak was a glowing pile of coals. It was evident from the expression on his face that he was shocked.

James, beaming proudly, told the old mountain man, "Guess you're a little surprised at how fast I work. When I start a job I don't waste time, do I?"

"You could say that," drawled Tom. "Ya did set some kind of record, I reckon. Yur a born logger, fer sure. But ya see, when I told ya I wanted the tree worked up I was expectin' somethin' a little different. See, I was plannin' to use that tree for my winter wood supply."

ERICKSON'S

In Portland's tough North End was located Erickson's Saloon. A sign over one door proclaimed it to be "The Workingmen's Club".

The outside of the building, which encompassed an entire city block, was rather dingy; but from the moment a logger elbowed his way in any of the five swinging doors his senses were rocked by the largest monument to alcohol the world has ever seen.

The centerpiece was a mirror-polished mahogany bar that circled the room, stretching 684 feet. One wall was dominated by "The Slave Market", a huge painting of voluptuous pink nudes captured by the legions of Rome. There was a concert stage where high-kicking chorus line girls performed; between acts the building vibrated to a grand pipe organ. A man could squander his bankroll at gaming tables scattered around the room or upstairs in curtained booths occupied by working girls.

Loggers fresh from the woods stood shoulder to shoulder along the great bar tossing down whiskey, two shots for a quarter, or beer at a nickel a mug. Any time of the day or night a man could avail himself of a gargantuan free lunch featuring thick-cut slices of homemade bread, juicy roast ox, sausage, Scandinavian cheeses, vats of pickled herring and quart jars of spicy mustard.

It was said that Erickson's Saloon was the true crossroad of the West and that if a man spent enough time there he would meet everyone he had ever known. Many friends kept in touch by tacking messages for one another on the enormous bulletin board.

The proprietor of the establishment was August Erickson. Over the years he made a staggering amount of money operating the world's most opulent saloon; but he was a free spender and gradually the hard-drinking, easy-losing workingmen of the frontier disappeared. August Erickson died penniless, a ward of the state of Oregon.

HIGH CLIMBER

In the early days of logging few jobs were as lonely or as dangerous as that of the high climber, the man who topped the trees to be used as spar poles. In some camps he also hung the rigging for cable logging.

The high climber was top man in any outfit, admired by his peers and paid a bonus for his extra risks. He climbed trees designated to become spar poles with long spurs and a safety belt he wrapped around the tree and flipped up as he climbed. Tied to him and dangling loose were a double-bit ax and a sharp saw which he used to cut all limbs as he came to them.

A high climber could be injured or killed in many ways. A misdirected ax blow could sever his safety belt. (In later years the core of the rope was made of steel, reducing this risk.) A gust of wind could whip the top of a tree and send a man flying to his death. Even after a tree was topped the swaying trunk could split; unless a climber were quick and dropped below the split he could be pinched to death between his rope and the tree.

One high climber who seemed to lead a charmed life was Tom Watson. He escaped death numerous times. One logger who worked with Tom on the Olympic Peninsula related the following story, "I was working in the woods with Tom the day he fell 120 feet. Saw him do it.

"He was going up a big fir when he lost his footing. Safety belt didn't hold. Tom came down, landed feet-first and sunk to about his knees in soft mud. The mud cushioned his fall. We pulled him out, sent him to town but the doc couldn't find anything wrong with him. So Tom, he put his clothes on and came back to work."

TRUE FRIENDS

It was the Christmas season but this was a sorrowful time as a young couple mourned the death of their four-month-old son.

Services were held in a skid shack at the logging camp. Rain drummed the tin roof. A fire snapped and crackled in a tin stove. The mother dabbed her eyes with a handkerchief and the father, an employee of the Long-Bell Lumber Company, stood like a statue showing no emotion. The congregation, composed of loggers and loggers' wives, sang a hymn about God and his loved ones being like jewels in a crown; and then the little white casket was carried to the car that served as a hearse.

At the cemetery four men, friends of the family, finished digging the grave. As the funeral procession approached they set their shovels aside and stepped forward. They carried the casket to the grave and stood through a brief ceremony. They were dressed in work clothes; brown duck jackets, brown duck trousers, rain hats and rubber boots. They had clay on their hands and clay on their boots. Rain made the soft clay run.

The white casket was lowered to its final resting place in a cedar box. The straps slid slowly through the calloused hands of the four men. The father and mother turned, walked away. The four men, true friends, remained behind to fill the grave. The rain continued to fall. Before morning it would snow.

TILLAMOOK BURN

August 14, 1933 was another hot, dry day in Oregon's coast range. By mid-morning humidity dropped to 22% and runners were sent out carrying orders that logging be suspended until fog or rain dampened the parched forest.

The bull buck heading the gypo operation in Gales Creek canyon northeast of Tillamook received the word and told his men to finish out the load, then shut down. The steam donkey pulled a giant Douglas fir over a windfall lying half-buried on the forest floor. As the wood ground together a spark dropped into a pile of dry leaves.

"Fire! Fire!" The call rang out. "Fire! Fire!" echoed off the canyon walls. Loggers tried frantically to contain the blaze with shovels, picks, axes, and finally dynamite. But the flames were fueled by a vast stand of virgin timber and there was no stopping them.

For ten days the fire burned and then, on August 24, a newspaper account related, "A great orange wall of flame eighteen miles across the front of the fire exploded out of the treetops. Many small fires became one enormous inferno, belching smoke and flame up, up, up into the heavens. A cloud forty miles wide mushroomed into the sky, to hang dull red, angry, and ominously over the blaze."

In one twenty-hour period the fire, which became known as the Tillamook Burn, devoured more than 12 billion board feet of prime timber, worth an estimated $250 million. Before rain arrived September 5 halting the fire, it had raged across 311,000 acres, burning the heart out of the greatest timber-producing state in the Union.

Within three months after the fire, with some of the snags still smoldering, crews went to work logging The Burn. They worked in knee-deep ash. There was no sweet smell of fir and cedar, only the stench of burned wood. There were no squirrels, no chipmunks scurrying around, no elk, no deer. The world was devoid of life. The trees stood as black skeletons in the foggy mist.

COMMERCIAL LOGGING

The first white man to fall a tree on the West Coast was a member of the crew of the pirate ship *Golden Hind*. In 1579, under tons of plunder and leaking badly at the seams, Sir Frances Drake ordered the ship be sailed into a protected inlet somewhere north of San Francisco Bay. Here a crew went ashore, chopped down trees and used the wood to repair their ship.

Two hundred years later British fur trading sea captain John Meares was the first to export logs from this region. He wrote in his journal, "We took on board a considerable quantity of fine spars, fir for topmasts, for the Chinese market, where they are very much wanted and of course proportionably dear. Indeed the woods of this part of America are capable of supplying with these valuable materials all the navies of Europe."

Commercial logging was launched in 1827 six miles up the Columbia River from Hudson's Bay Company's Fort Vancouver. Chief Factor Dr. John McLoughlin, needing lumber to build boxes for shipping furs to England, imported a mechanical saw driven by water power and capable of cutting 3,000 board feet of lumber per day.

In addition to boxes the lumber was also used in construction at Fort Vancouver and some was exported to Hawaii (known then as the Sandwich Islands). Until the Oregon Trail was opened in 1843, bringing in a flood of pioneers and creating a local market, lumber was produced on a small scale.

The real boom for West Coast wood products began in 1848 with the discovery of gold in California. At that time the entire West Coast was producing only 25 million board feet of lumber annually; a decade later production topped 300 million board feet. Most of the lumber was sold in California but toward the latter part of the 1800s fleets of sailing ships were exporting lumber from the West Coast to ports throughout the world.

THE ACCIDENT

Logger Harold Morgan talks about the accident, saying, "It was July 6, 1944, the day before my 29th birthday.

"Was working high lead. Cable should have been on a guy and shackle but it wasn't, was on the ground. Second pull it caught me, knocked me into a stump, broke my neck. Guess the boys packed me to the landing, put me in the back of a pickup.

"I came to in the hospital. Asked one of the boys who brought me in -- all I could do was whisper -- if he had taken my boots off. Didn't want to die with my corks on.

" 'Am I going to make it?' I asked and he says, 'Hell yes, you'll make it.' Felt a little better after that except I was paralyzed from my neck down and after the shock started to wear off the hurting started. Oh, my God, did I hurt!

"My brothers came in and stayed with me. One time when they thought I was asleep I heard one of them crying and he said, 'Poor little guy will never live to see morning light.' But I toughed it out. Finally, on about the third day, I moved my thumb on my right hand, wiggled it back and forth a couple of times and then and there I knew I'd live.

"There was some terrible times. Terrible pain. Got hooked on morphine and dreamed I was being chased by stumps and flailing roots. They dried me out, sent me home. I was in such a bad way I almost committed suicide. Had the gun up to my head, safety off and then realized what I was doing and it scared me so bad I sold the gun.

"And then my wife, she couldn't cope with the situation and pulled out leaving me with the two children, a boy, six, and a girl, four. The night she left she told me, 'I married you to get away from home. I never did love you.' Told her, 'Thanks a lot, Honey.'

"Got to where I could get around with a cane and went to work at the Wolf Point lookout on the summit of the Coast range. Took the kids up there with me. They were raised there, 23 seasons, and they turned out all right."

53

CAT IN THE TENT

A road crew was building logging roads in the Coast range the summer of 1927. Their headquarters was a church at the mouth of Daniels Creek, the sanctuary made the dining room and the parsonage served as a bunkhouse.

One weekend a fellow named Peart invited his young son and daughter to spend the night and have Sunday dinner with him. The children arrived late in the afternoon and were bubbling with excitement at having come so deep in the woods and the prospect of sleeping in a tent beside the church. But near bedtime the boy hesitantly wanted to know, "Pa, are there any wild animals in these here parts?"

"Naw," his father reassured him. "Back in the woods you'll find an occasional wild animal, but they stay away from here."

That night the boy lay awake long after everyone else was asleep. He listened to his sister's measured breathing from the bunk near him and the snoring of the men inside the parsonage. Finally he began to feel drowsy. His eyes reluctantly closed.

While he slept a cougar padded silently into the clearing, attracted by pies set in an open window for Sunday dinner. A dog in camp smelled the cougar, howled and gave chase. The cougar wheeled and bounded through the children's open tent flaps. The dog followed and total pandemonium broke loose inside the tent.

It was over as quickly as it began. The cougar found the exit and leaped through it with the dog in hot pursuit. The dog treed the cougar and at first light the loggers shot the cat out of the tree. They offered the pelt to Peart's children but they declined.

LAST LOAD

"Gonna be a cold winter," announced Curtis Parker to his wife that November day in 1900. "Think I'll get another load of wood."

Curtis hitched his team to the wagon, threw an ax and a saw in back and invited his oldest son to come along. As they departed, Curtis's wife and the other seven children stood on the porch of their homestead cabin and waved goodby. Curtis reassured them, "We'll be home before dark."

It was snowing lightly as the team pulled the wagon into the foothills of the Blue Mountains. When they reached timber Curtis and his son left the team and wagon and hiked up the hillside, searching for a standing snag with dry wood. They found one and Curtis went to work falling it, sending the boy down the hill to bring up the team.

The snag was on the ground and the horses hitched to it. Curtis handed the saw to his boy and warned, "Carry this but be careful. Make sure the teeth point away from you. If you slip, get rid of it. Falling on a saw can be mighty dangerous."

Curtis stuck his double-bitted ax in the top of the log and started the team with a pop of the reins and a click. "Move. Let's go."

The work team pulled, snaking the log downhill over a skift of snow. Perhaps the log hung on a rock, throwing Curtis off balance. No one ever knew for sure what happened except that Curtis fell or was thrown onto the ax and it cut deeply into his thigh severing the artery.

"Come here! Quick!" called Curtis.

Curtis Parker, the pioneer, the homesteader, the husband and father, lay on the powder white snow and within a few short minutes he bled to death.

THE BARREL

James Steward was a professional daredevil who billed himself as Captain Webb. On the 4th of July, 1895 he was hired to perform a stunt for the loggers at Rosen's Camp near Coeur D'Alene, Idaho. He was going to run the company log chute in a barrel.

Five hundred loggers gathered to watch as Captain Webb made a last-minute inspection of the wooden barrel, a homemade affair shaped like a cigar and measuring two feet in diameter and six feet six inches in length.

"Are you scared?" someone asked.

"Scared?" repeated the captain. "Not in the least. This is a piece of cake. In fact, I'm so confident nothing will go wrong, I'll dispense with the harness." He removed the restraining device, tossed it on the deck and squeezed himself into the narrow tube. The lid was closed.

Several men pushed the barrel to get it started. Inside Captain Webb took a quick breath and reassured himself that within a few quick minutes he would be splashing safely into the mill pond.

The barrel shot forward, riding the chute as it descended a steep slope over the edge of a canyon wall. Near the halfway point was a rock outcropping and the chute was built with a slight incline to clear it before plunging to the pond. It was at this point that the barrel, traveling at a terrifying speed, became airborne. It left the chute, shot over the trestle and crashed onto the rocks below.

When rescuers reached the point of impact they found the barrel split open and the captain bleeding badly and clinging to a sliver of life. In a weak voice he managed to speak, telling the loggers, "Guess I should've strapped myself in." Those were his last words.

PICTURES FOR PROOF

The summer of 1905 two college boys, Hugh Sparks and James Ward, started a photography business.

With a hack and a rundown team they traveled east of the Cascades, stopping at logging camps and sawmills to photograph the crews. The film was processed on the spot and photographs were sold to the men.

The enterprising youths also stopped at scattered homesteads and if the homesteader had money or something to trade, the family would be lined up and their photograph taken. Business was unbelievably good. Then one day a masked man armed with a rifle leaped off an embankment into the middle of the road and demanded, "Reach for the sky! Toss me the bag."

"What bag?" Hugh wanted to know.

"Don't be stupid. The money bag. Give it here."

James kept one hand in the air while he reached with the other under the seat. He brought out the bag that held the $50 they had collected and tossed it on the ground. The masked man, keeping the rifle trained on the boys, reached and retrieved the bag. He turned and started up the embankment but lost his footing and fell.

With startling quickness James grabbed the wagon whip, leaped from the seat and brought the butt of the whip down over the masked man's head. The man dropped his rifle and sunk to his knees. While he was stunned James and Hugh tied him up, unmasked him and took photographs just in case he managed to escape.

They delivered the thief to the front door of the county jail. That fall they returned to Pacific University with pockets full of money, a great story to tell and pictures to prove it.

MODERN LOGGER

Lumberjacks originated in Maine. They cut the white pine and when it was gone they swept into New York and Pennsylvania before moving on to the Great Lakes states. They fell government timber and then drove the red men from the reservations and fell the reservation timber.

Near the turn of the twentieth century the lumberjacks came west to northern California and the Pacific Northwest to log the straightest, biggest, thickest timber any of them had ever seen.

In the wake of the loggers came farmers to grub stumps and plant fields. Skidroads became highways and towns were platted. The lumberjacks' ancient enemy, civilization, had caught up to them.

As the West became developed the citizens of the towns and cities demanded that the forests be set aside for recreation. There was no room for the old adage of "Cut Out and Get Out!".

The hard-shelled lumberjack and timber baron gave way to a young generation of foresters who spoke of safety, conservation, selective logging, sustained yield and believed timber should be grown and harvested like a crop. Unlike their fathers and grandfathers whose purpose in life was to cut as much timber as possible, as fast as possible, and get it to the mill quickly and cheaply; this new generation realized it had an obligation to the public and the environment.

The loggers and lumbermen of today use advances in technology to protect the environment and reduce any impact on the forest. They look to the future to remedy the wastefulness of the past.

Rick Steber's Tales of the Wild West Series is available in hardbound books ($14.95) and paperback books ($4.95) featuring illustrations by Don Gray, as well as in audio tapes ($7.95) narrated by Dallas McKennon. Current titles in the series include —

OREGON TRAIL Vol. 1 *
PACIFIC COAST Vol. 2 *
INDIANS Vol. 3 *
COWBOYS Vol. 4 *
WOMEN OF THE WEST Vol. 5 *
CHILDREN'S STORIES Vol. 6 *
LOGGERS Vol. 7 *
MOUNTAIN MEN Vol. 8 *
MINERS Vol. 9 *
GRANDPA'S STORIES Vol. 10
PIONEERS Vol. 11
CAMPFIRE STORIES Vol. 12
TALL TALES Vol. 13
GUNFIGHTERS Vol. 14
GRANDMA'S STORIES Vol. 15

*Available on Audio Tape

Other books written by Rick Steber —

ROUNDUP
LAST OF THE PIONEERS
HEARTWOOD
WHERE ROLLS THE OREGON

NEW YORK TO NOME
WILD HORSE RIDER
TRACES
RENDEZVOUS

If unavailable at retailers in your area write directly to the publisher. A catalog is free upon request.

Bonanza Publishing
Box 204
Prineville, Oregon 97754